D1303519

THE BOY, THE FARMER

*To my Mother. She taught me that learning,
if embraced, will be a lifelong friend. . . .*

She typed our papers, while packing eight lunches.

Tutored us, while cooking for ten.

*Taught us that praying starts with gratitude,
while selling Grandma's silver.*

*Checked homework, and tucked us in,
after waiting tables on Mother's Day.*

*And to my incredible wife, who will be proud, and happy,
that I finished this book, and dedicated it to my mother.*

Published by JaB Publishers in 2014

Printed in the USA

Manufactured by Thomson-Shore, Dexter, MI (USA); RMA35DK24, December, 2014

ISBN: 978-0-692-31493-7

JaB Publishers, LLC
3 West End Avenue
Old Greenwich, CT 06870

To order additional copies, visit
www.Back40mercantile.com

————————————————

"My mother had a great deal of trouble with me
but I think she enjoyed it."

— Mark Twain

THE BOY,
THE FARMER

By Jeffrey Kane Bischoff

Illustrations by John Gummere
Edited by Benjamin Brassord

Every day, rain or shine, the Boy woke before his seven siblings and tiptoed outside to start his paper route. He liked pedaling his shiny red bike through the early morning quiet as the sun gently woke the birds and squirrels. The first house he went to was an old farmhouse, with a giant maple tree in front. He knew the Farmer would be waiting for him.

In 1994, 57% of newspaper carriers were under age eighteen, and typically boys. Adults in cars now make up 81% of the country's newspaper deliverers. Many mourn the lost sense of community that came with the paperboy. (1)

The Farmer's kitchen light was always on, and sometimes, the Boy could see the Farmer hunched over his coffee. The Boy would let the storm door slam a little so the Farmer knew the paper had arrived.

They never spoke. The Farmer lived alone except for a couple of big old sheep dogs that followed him wherever he went.

New England dairy farmers woke before the sun to get a jump on their busy days. The cows needed to be milked in the morning, and at night, every day, never a holiday. The milk needed to be bottled, chilled, and sold, after the cream was pulled off the top. The farmers' wives and daughters made cheese, butter, pies and breads and had to prepare three enormous meals daily. It was estimated that colonial era farmers burned more calories than today's long distance runners.

The Farmer had a tough life. He worked every day, rain or shine. People said he hadn't smiled since his wife died.

Every week on collection day, the Farmer would leave a crumpled up dollar bill, or some coins, as payment for the newspapers in the small mustard colored envelope that the boy would clip to the paper. Every once in a while, the Farmer would leave some maple sugar candy for the Boy.

Early American farmers had to be expert hunters, trappers, timber framers, lumberjacks, mechanics, veterinarians and sometimes soldiers. The farmers spent their winters working in the barn, inventing and crafting tools that would allow them to work smarter and faster. Necessity has always been the mother of invention. Not much has changed for today's farmers, but they have the previous generations of farmers to thank for so many innovations that make their lives "easier."

Every spring the Farmer would drive his red tractor up and down the field planting the corn, seed by seed, in perfect rows. The Boy admired him because he knew how hard it was to grow corn. He would sit on the stonewall for hours and watch the Farmer work his fields.

Sometimes the Farmer would look over at the Boy and nod his head towards him. The Farmer spent most of the day on his tractor, sometimes with the rain dripping off the brim of his hat.

In the spring, after the maple trees had been tapped, and the sap boiled to syrup, the fields needed to be plowed and planted. In the summer the farmers cultivated until the crops were tall enough to shade out the weeds. In the fall they harvested and put up hay. The barns needed to be filled with hay, the cupboards filled with smoked meat, winter squash, pumpkins, pickles, and flour. From the last snowfall to the first snowfall they prepared their homesteads for winter. An average colonial family burned 40 cords of wood per year. A cord is 128 cubic feet (4 feet by 4 feet by 8 feet). Farmers had a tradition of planting two maple trees in front of their newly built farmhouses. They are called "husband and wife trees."

The Boy loved to watch the corn grow as the long summer days and rains fed the plants. It would always be knee high by the 4th of July! Then the tassels would appear, then the silks! He knew it would not be long until he would be eating corn on the cob smothered in melted butter.

And finally, the Farmer would set up an old wooden table outside his house, next to the stonewall, and put out bushels of the sweetest corn the Boy ever tasted.

Corn, like every crop, competes with weeds, and since pesticides are a modern invention, the hand cultivating of crops was always near the top of the priority list for early American farmers. Corn needed to be properly spaced so as to allow for hand hoeing, horse drawn cultivating, or in the modern age of tractors, mechanized multi-row cultivating. Corn, as seen in frames 3 and 4, is wind pollinated from the tassels on the top to the silks on the ears. Each single strand of silk attaches to its own individual kernel. America planted 97 million acres of corn in 2013 and harvested enough to fill 650 full-sized college football stadiums. (2)

There was an old metal box to put the money in, and a pile of tattered burlap bags to put the corn in. The Boy's Mother would buy as many as she could afford. The corn always sold out within a few hours.

Nobody ever spoke to the Farmer; the neighborhood kids said he was a mean man. The Boy felt that wasn't true because of the maple sugar candy, and the way the Farmer played with his sheep dogs.

Many small farmers still rely on the honor system. Their time is precious and they have been raised in a handshake-agreement culture. The extent of written contracts in their fathers' and grandfathers' lives consisted of three letters: I.O.U. Many people interviewed regarding the psychology of the honor system have reported a positive emotion when given an opportunity to be trusted.

S ometimes the Boy's Mother struggled to feed her eight children. The Boy's brothers and sisters turned over any money they made from babysitting, shoveling snow, and raking leaves to help their Mother and Father buy groceries.

The Boy's favorite meal was mashed potatoes and corn, with cold watermelon for dessert.

Given the potato's versatility and commercial value, farmers typically grew them in abundance. The potato keeps well in a root cellar. It can be prepared in a multitude of ways. It can make pie, bread, even spirits. The Irish potato famine (now termed "The Great Hunger") from 1845-1852 killed approximately 1 million people and caused another 1 million Irish to emigrate, mostly to the United States. Almost 40 million Americans trace their ancestry to the island of Ireland. (3)

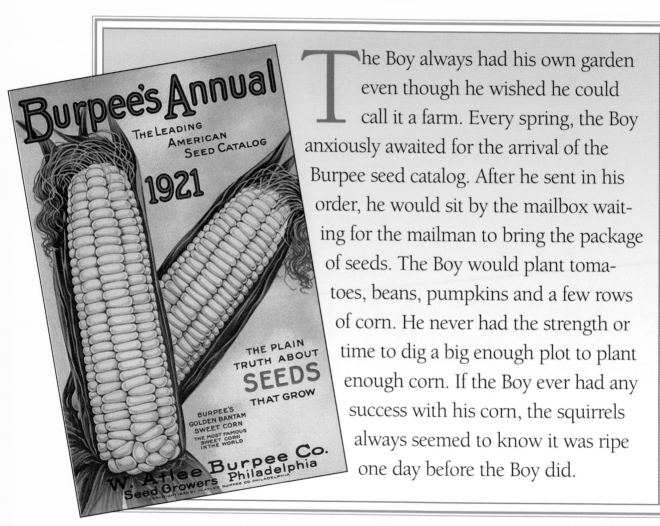

The Boy always had his own garden even though he wished he could call it a farm. Every spring, the Boy anxiously awaited for the arrival of the Burpee seed catalog. After he sent in his order, he would sit by the mailbox waiting for the mailman to bring the package of seeds. The Boy would plant tomatoes, beans, pumpkins and a few rows of corn. He never had the strength or time to dig a big enough plot to plant enough corn. If the Boy ever had any success with his corn, the squirrels always seemed to know it was ripe one day before the Boy did.

One Saturday morning in April, the mailman brought the package from Burpee's. In it was an enormous bag of corn seeds, much more than the Boy had ever ordered before. The Boy's Mother asked him how he could have paid for this much corn seed, and she wanted to know what he was going to do with it all.

"Momma," the Boy said, "I have been saving my newspaper money and this year I am going to grow a big cornfield. I want to be a Farmer, not a gardener. I am tired of growing squirrel corn. I want us to have a lot of corn, enough to sell, so we can buy a new waffle maker. I love waffles."

The Burpee company was founded in Philadelphia in 1876 by an eighteen year old with a passion for plants and animals and a mother willing to lend him $1,000 in "seed money" to get started. Within 25 years he had developed the largest seed company in America. By 1915 they were mailing a million catalogs a year to America's victory gardeners. Victory gardens were planted at private residences and public parks in America during the two World Wars. About one third of the vegetables in the United States came from victory gardens. Besides indirectly aiding the war effort, these gardens were considered a morale booster in that gardeners could feel empowered by their contribution of labor and were rewarded by their produce grown. (4)

The next day, the Boy got up early, like every day, and delivered his newspapers. When he was done, he went out back and started digging. If he wanted to turn his garden into a farm he would need to turn over an awful lot of heavy sod. That would be even harder than snow shoveling after a big storm. He outlined his new plot with some string and got to work.

After digging for most of the day, the Boy realized he was going to have to work for 100 days to turn his garden into a farm. He sat down, hands blistered, beside his garden that was not a farm . . . and he cried.

Native Americans implemented a farming technique commonly referred to as the Three Sisters. It is the inter-planting of corn, beans, and squash on the same plot of land. It has been proven to be a highly sustainable method of farming given the symbiotic relationship among the three plants. Beans provide nitrogen to the soil, the corn stalks provide a pole for the beans to climb, and the squash leaves provide shade to keep out the weeds and help maintain the soil's moisture. Coincidentally, the author also has three sisters. (5)

Suddenly, the Boy heard the familiar noise of the Farmer's tractor. The Boy stood up and was surprised to see the Farmer as he drove onto his lawn, past the rope swing, over the stone path and right into the garden. The tractor's engine was so loud the Boy's family came running out of the house to see what was going on. Smoke billowed out of the tractor as it dragged the plow through the heavy sod, cutting it like a hot knife through butter. Within ten minutes the Boy's garden became a farm.

Farmall tractors were a mass-produced, multi-purpose tractor manufactured in Illinois from the 1920s to the 1970s (the brand has recently made a comeback and has a loyal following among antique tractor collectors). The Farmall was so versatile that it almost entirely replaced the farmers' need for horses. It had high ground clearance, excellent visibility all around the machine, sufficient power for plowing and harrowing, a belt pulley that enabled the farmer to deliver what amounted to electricity anywhere on his farm. He could run a saw mill, threshing machine, water pump, conveyor belt, using a long leather belt fastened to a free-spinning wheel powered by the tractor's motor. Saving labor hours enabled farms to become more efficient, more innovative, and more profitable. The Farmall is credited as leading that progress.

As the Farmer drove his tractor back towards the street, he slowed down long enough to look over at the Boy and tip his hat . . . and smile. At that moment, the Boy knew, without a doubt, that the Farmer was a nice man.

In 1939, an average tractor had approximately 30 horsepower and cost $1,100. Today's state-of-the-art tractor can come with up to 600 horsepower and can cost more than $500,000. With that increase of power has come speed and efficiency. The corn yield per acre on a farm in 1939 compared to a farm in 2014 has gone from 63 bushels per acre to 171.7 bushels per acre. (6)

After the smoke had cleared, the Boy's Mother walked over and put her arm around him and said "Jeffrey, you are a great newspaper boy. Now you can be a great Farmer."

THE END

About the Author

This is a true story. Completely true.

I am the middle of eight children. Well, I share that "status" with my younger brother Warren. We grew up in the town of Old Saybrook, Connecticut. The house in which this story played out is on the Old Boston Post Road. The Post Road is a very historic road, with many different branches; some of which were actually converted Indian paths . . . we lived on the southern leg that went from New York to Boston, by way of Providence, along the Connecticut coast. Our house was built in the mid 19th century. It sure was big, and old. The floors creaked when you walked up the stairs holding onto the hand worn banister. There was this really cool, very narrow and dark, servants' staircase in the back that went from our kitchen to a small bedroom. We didn't have any servants.

I love history, don't you?

Studying it, exploring it . . . looking at an 18th century stonewall immediately makes me think of the farmers who placed each rock in its eternal resting place. Did you know that a "rock" becomes a "stone" as soon as it becomes useful?

We know the stonewall was built to clear the field after the farmer harvested all the wood. When the settlers showed up, all of New England was covered in old growth forests — an enormous discovery when you consider Europe's forests had long since been exploited, almost to extinction. A New World homestead was built by felling and hewing trees; it was heated by firewood that was harvested by hand and ax. The fires were lit in the fall and stoked around the clock, through the entire winter.

Did you know that if the stonewall had small stones in it, that meant the adjoining field was used for crops? (Farmers wouldn't care about removing small stones if the field was an animal pasture.) Did you know that a lace wall signified that the field was used as a sheep pasture? (Sheep are excellent climbers, but are afraid to climb a wall that they think will crumble on them.)

I didn't learn this until I read *Stone by Stone* and *Exploring Stone Walls* by Robert Thorson.

The author, 1972, in his cornfield, Old Saybrook, Connecticut

Who else taught me cool stuff?

My friend, terrestrial ecologist, historian, author, college professor, forest detective, conservation activist, my idol, Tom Wessels.

You should go read his book *Reading the Forested Landscape*. Why? Because you'll be able to understand what a "pillow" in a forest is. I don't want to spoil the surprise.

What did Robert and Tom teach me? How much time do we have?

In the 1850's, New Englanders cleared 75% of their forests to create sheep pastures. It wasn't long before those pastures started growing stones and rocks, freed and forced upwards by the freeze and thaw process . . . inching towards the top like bubbles climbing to the under surface of a frozen pond. Crack the ice and the bubble gets freed up, just like the rock rising up from the spot the last glacier left it, 20,000 years ago. What to do with all the rocks? The farmers made stonewalls, thus eliminating the need to use all that good firewood keeping sheep in, or hogs out.

We definitely grow rocks in the Northeast. Try this: clear a big garden patch, or a farm field, of every rock bigger than an apple.

Wait one year and come back. You'll be surprised to learn that the field has sprouted and "grown" a whole new crop of rocks. We call them "New England potatoes."

Why do we care about all of this stuff? The real question is why WOULDN'T we care! If you aren't curious . . . you won't live a fulfilling life. My mother taught me that. She gave me the best gift I ever got: Eric Sloane's *Diary of an Early American Boy*. I still have the copy that she gave me after a 1972 visit to Sturbridge Village (My Mecca). (Don't tell my brothers; they thought it was lost during one of our 22 moves.)

You definitely need to buy that book . . . and if you like seasons as much as I do, go buy Sloane's *Seasons of America Past*; you have to trust me on this! My life was profoundly shaped by the writings and sketches of Eric Sloane. I don't know when I fell in love with the seasons; I think it may have been 1967. I was five years old and found crocuses peeking through the melting snow, ushering in Spring. I love each season equally. Maple syrup, rope swings, pumpkins, and snowmen.

My brothers and I were wild kids . . . perhaps I'll use the modern diagnosis: "spirited." We were spirited boys.

Our mother would kick her children out of the house in the morning with the loving instructions: "don't come back unless someone's bleeding."

If we got really hungry, and the blackberry bushes were empty, we would draw straws to see who had to make himself bleed. Unless of course one of us was already conveniently bleeding from "natural" causes.

A snow storm meant a chance to make some big snowmen, and some big money . . . my brothers and I would grab our shovels and go door to door. Our sisters babysat for their "spending money." Spending was defined as giving the money to Mom and Dad for groceries and keeping a little to spend at Patrick's Country Store. I loved Bazooka bubble gum, black licorice, and maple sugar. I would trade a fishing pole for maple sugar!

Our parents stressed education. We played geography games with a globe that was so wobbly you had to hold it with both hands in order to point to Vietnam with your nose.

Fun times. No time to notice we were hungry.

The farmer who lived down the street from us was a mysterious man, exactly as I describe him in the book you just read.

It remains a mystery as to who asked the farmer to plow my garden into a farm. He just showed up one day . . . chugging and smoking and churning earth, completely unannounced and uninvited. To this day, I can smell the fumes and see the sod turning over, but his face is blurry; it was more than 40 years ago.

Neither one of my parents recalls asking him.

The author, 2013

I would hug that farmer if I ever saw him again. I hold farmers in very high regard; you should too.

I looked for the farm a decade ago; it had disappeared. You can't go back. Always forward.

Mom lives nearby. Dad passed away in 2012. Lesley owns the Back 40 Farm; Greg runs the property. Rich, Lia, Nick, and Warren all live between DC and Martha's Vineyard. Rachel lives in Burlington, Vermont, my third favorite state after Connecticut and California. We all graduated from college, thanks to Mom (she has 21 grandchildren).

Every Thanksgiving we converge on the farm for a long weekend of overeating and over sharing.

Life is good, but it seems the days turn into nights faster than they did in 1972. Time definitely flies, which is why we read . . . and explore . . . and learn as fast as we can.

And if we're really fortunate? We'll get to teach, and mentor, and guide . . . and entertain.

Let me run . . . I'm writing a book about a boy, and a stonewall, and this chipmunk who teaches him a valuable lesson.

I don't want to spoil the surprise.

I am blessed to be married to the most amazing woman I've ever met . . . my little Greek koukla, Katrina. And my sun rises and sets on the foreheads of our two children, Warren and Marianna . . . they make us prouder and prouder every day.

— Jeffrey Kane Bischoff
October 14, 2014, Old Greenwich, CT

About the Illustrator

As a boy, the closest I got to farming was growing tomatoes and mint in my backyard in Trenton, New Jersey.

My mother was well known in our area as the "go-to" portrait painter, and art was always a way of life for me. I majored in Architecture at Columbia University, but my first love was painting and drawing. For my day job after college I worked in printing, graphic design and illustration, and later returned to school at the Pennsylvania Academy of the Fine Arts, where I graduated from the four-year Certificate Program in Painting in 1996. I exhibit my oil paintings in galleries and elsewhere around the Middle Atlantic states. This is my third book for young readers.

In my other life I work with the Philadelphia-Serengeti Alliance, a new nonprofit organization focused on developing water resources in Tanzania — we have finished our first well and have more in the works! I have two daughters and one stepdaughter, and live in South Philadelphia with my wife Sue. I'll enjoy reading *The Boy, The Farmer* with my granddaughter.

With my illustrations for Jeffrey's book I would like to honor the memory of my sister, Mary Gummere Hall, who loved people, art and New England.

You can see more of my work at www.be.net/JohnGummere.

Bibliography

1. http://content.time.com/time/magazine/article/0,9171,2046070,00.html

2. http://www.nass.usda.gov/Newsroom/2013/06_28_2013.asp

3. http://www.britannica.com/EBchecked/topic/294137/Irish-Potato-Famine

4. http://www.burpee.com/gardening/content/company-history/history.html)

5. http://blogs.cornell.edu/garden/get-activities/signature-projects/the-three-sisters-exploring-an-iroquois-garden/how-to-plant-the-three-sisters/

6. http://cornandsoybeandigest.com/blog/usda-projects-record-2014-crop-production)